charles

by S. E. HUME • Illustrations by JESSICA BROMLEY BARTRAM

Fitzhenry & Whiteside

Published in Canada by Fitzhenry & Whiteside, 195 Allstate Parkway, Markham, ON L3R 4T8
Published in the United States by Fitzhenry & Whiteside, 311 Washington Street, Brighton, MA 02135
www.fitzhenry.ca
10 9 8 7 6 5 4 3 2 1

Fitzhenry & Whiteside acknowledges with thanks the Canada Council for the Arts and
the Ontario Arts Council for their support of our publishing program.

Canada Council **Conseil des Arts**
for the Arts **du Canada**

ONTARIO ARTS COUNCIL
CONSEIL DES ARTS DE L'ONTARIO
an Ontario government agency
un organisme du gouvernement de l'Ontario

Hume, Stephen, 1947-, author
Charles / S.E. Hume ; Jessica Bartram.
ISBN 978-1-55455-416-4 (hardcover)
I. Bartram, Jessica, 1985-, illustrator II. Title.
PS8565.U555C43 2017   C813'.54   C2017-905987-4
Publisher Cataloging-in-Publication Data (U.S.)

Names: Hume, Stephen Easton, 1947-, author. | Bartram, Jessica Bromley, illustrator.
Title: Charles / by S. E. Hume; illustrations by Jessica Bromley Bartram.
Description: Markham, Ontario: Fitzhenry & Whiteside, 2017. | Summary: A young girl finds an injured crow that she nurses back to
health. The time comes for him to leave, but he brings a "sweet" message for the girl who took care of him.
Identifiers: ISBN 978-1-55455-416-4 (hardcover)
Subjects: LCSH: Crows – Juvenile fiction. | Wildlife rescue -- Juvenile fiction. | Farewells – Juvenile fiction.
| BISAC: JUVENILE FICTION / Animals / Birds.
Classification: LCC PZ7.H864Ch | DDC [E] – dc23

Cover and interior design by Kerry Plumley
Printed in China by Sheck Wah Tong Printing Press Ltd

This book is for Steve Chin.

S.E.H.

To my parents—thank you for
encouraging my love of nature.

J.B.B.

This is a drawing of Charles,
my crow.

He used to live in my house.

I will never forget the first time I saw him.

He was sitting on a pile of leaves,
almost bald, looking around at the big new world.

CHARLES CHARLES CHA
CHARLES CHA
CHARLES CHAR
CHARLES
CHARLES CHARLES
ARLES CHARLES CHA
ARLES

I came back that evening and he was still there.
He needed help.

He was making a funny noise.
It sounded like, "Charles."

I picked Charles up and brought
him home.

I put him in a shoebox lined
with old newspapers and
comic books I didn't read anymore.

I fed Charles cooked cereal. I fed him scrambled eggs.

I mashed up strawberries in the cereal. He liked that.

I hung a light bulb above the box to keep him warm.

Charles walked before
he learned how to fly.

He followed me everywhere,
with small, sideways steps.

Charles grew. His feathers and eyes
were as black as the midnight.

He liked to sit on my shoulder when
I wrote and tap my shiny fountain pen
with his beak.

It was hard to write like that.
My sentences looked like this.

We grew strawberries in our backyard.

Sometimes my mother would send me to collect berries for dinner.

After a while, Charles
started flying from our house
to the big pine tree at the
edge of the woods.

My mother and father said it would not
be too long before he returned to his true
home in the wild woods.

One morning, Charles was gone.

"It was only a matter of time,"
my mother said.

"Yes," my father said.
"He probably missed the outdoors."

That day, I stood outside and called him.
There was no answer.

But one night, many nights later,
I was in my room. I couldn't sleep.

There was a full moon outside.
Suddenly, I heard taps on my window.
A big black crow was sitting on the
ledge with a strawberry in his beak.

When I got up to see if it was Charles,
the bird flew away.

But he left the strawberry.

It was the sweetest berry I ever tasted.